J   Minahan, John A.,
Minahan   1956-

          Abigail's drum.

Abigail's Drum

JOHN A. MINAHAN

Abigail's Drum

illustrations by **Robert Quackenbush**

 **Pippin Press**
New York

Published by Pippin Press, 229 East 85th Street
Gracie Station Box 1347
New York, N.Y. 10028

Printed in Hong Kong
10 9 8 7 6 5 4 3 2 1

Library of Congress Cataloging-in-Publication Data

Minahan, John A., 1956–
    Abigail's drum / by John A. Minahan; drawings by Robert
Quackenbush.
        p.   cm.
    Summary: During the War of 1812, when British soldiers threaten
the town of Scituate, Massachusetts, young Rebecca Bates and her
sister, Abigail, daughters of the local lighthouse keeper, find a way
to save both him and the town.
    ISBN 0–945912–25–0
    1. United States—History—War of 1812—Juvenile fiction.
[1. United States—History—War of 1812—Fiction.   2. Lighthouses-
-Fiction.]   I. Quackenbush, Robert M., ill.   II. Title.
PZ7.M65163Ab   1995
[Fic]—dc 20   95–23460
                                                                    CIP
                                                                    AC

To my family

J.A.M.

1 Rescue

Contents

Rebecca Bates stood on the stony beach near Scituate Lighthouse. A cool wind blew salt spray into her face. The sun had just set and darkness was gathering on the ocean. She smiled. Supper was finished, the kitchen was cleaned up, and chores were done for the moment. Finally, she could play her fife. She raised the little wooden instrument to her lips and sent a song out over the waves.

The fife was a gift from her father, who had brought it home from one of his voyages when he had been a sea captain. She had taught herself to play, with much encouragement from her parents. Music was important to everyone in the Bates family. Ma sang, Pa played the fiddle, and Abigail, Rebecca's younger sister, had a small drum, also a gift from Pa. Abigail could bang out a simple rhythm with a pair of drumsticks while Pa sawed away at his lively tunes.

Lately, though, the lighthouse had taken all of Pa's time—and chores had taken all of Rebecca's. That was why she liked to practice here on the beach. Anywhere else, someone was sure to find something for her to do.

In a few minutes, when she was halfway through one of her favorite tunes, Rebecca heard the door on the gray, shingled cottage behind her bang open and shut. Pa was coming to light the lamps in the lighthouse.

She put down the fife. "I'm on my way," she called automatically. Being eleven years old, she was expected to help with housework and to lend a hand in the lighthouse. She had been working especially hard this week, since her mother had gone up to Boston to care for a sick cousin.

Rebecca didn't mind chores, exactly. But music showed her that there was more to life than sweeping and polishing and dusting, and she wished she had more time for it.

"It's a fine evening, Rebecca," Pa called back as he lowered the flag from its pole near the lighthouse. "You can play one more tune before you come up."

He folded the flag and headed for the storage

shed that connected the cottage and the octagonal white tower. The entrance to the lighthouse was just inside the shed's door, and soon Rebecca could hear Pa climbing to the lamp-room. Sounds echoed around inside the hollow stone shaft of the lighthouse, then shot out a big hatchway that faced the sea near the bottom, opened to let in fresh air. Each step Pa took cracked like a gunshot.

Rebecca began playing again. Gulls cawed in the darkening sky. Waves crashed and, hissing on pebbles, withdrew back into the sea. The lighthouse stood at the end of a finger of land called Cedar Point, so Rebecca saw nothing but the great darkness of the Atlantic Ocean.

Somewhere out there, battles were being fought. It was September of 1812, and America was at war with England again. Although the Revolutionary War had ended nearly thirty years ago with the United States winning its independence, most Americans felt that England had never stopped trying to control their new country, and another war had started this summer. Pa had explained it to his daughters, adding that many sailors from here in Massachusetts were fighting the British. But it all seemed complicated and far away to them.

13

The top of the lighthouse lit up, and soon the glow got brighter. That meant Pa was busy going from one lamp to the next, lighting each in turn. It was time for Rebecca to climb up there and polish all the glass and brass in the lamp-room. Sighing, she tucked the fife into the pocket of her apron and picked her way toward the tower. It was slow going, since the beach was covered with loose rocks smoothed and rounded by the waves.

When she heard an urgent ringing from over-head she stopped and looked up. Pa stood on the railed porch that ran around the top of the light-house. He was clanging the small fog bell mounted on a short stand up there.

"What is it, Pa?" she called.

He pointed to the ocean.

Rebecca squinted. The glow of the lamps created a halo around the tower, turning the water milky and making distant objects hard to see. Into that halo floated a dory. The one-man fishing boat was heading toward the big boulders off the tip of Cedar Point. The sail on its mast was bellied out with wind.

Pa waved his arms over his head. The light behind him threw his long, wild shadow across the water. He rang the bell again but the dory still headed for the rocks.

Pa vanished back inside. The clatter of his footsteps hurrying down the tower came shooting out the hatchway. Rebecca ran to meet him at the shed's door.

"The bell did no good," Pa said, not sounding surprised. He had often complained that the lighthouse's builders should have arranged for a larger, louder fog bell down on the ground. "We'll have to fire a warning," he added.

Rebecca rushed inside and helped him roll a signal cannon past the barrels of whale oil that fueled the lamps. Once they got the tiny cannon out into the open, they aimed it toward the water. Rebecca covered her ears while Pa took a box of wooden matches from a pocket in his shirt. He struck one and touched the fuse. Spitting smoke and fire, the cannon let out a huge, bone-jarring roar. For a moment the reek of burned powder hung in the air. Then the breeze cleared the smoke.

The dory was still coming. By now Rebecca could see a figure hunched over in the boat. Above the breaking of waves came another sound—the screech of wood against rock. The boat had struck the boulders.

"I'll have to row out," Pa said.

They had often drilled for this kind of emergency, so Rebecca knew that she should have been checking the rope they used as a lifeline, making sure it was coiled neatly with its end knotted to a post near the tower. But fright kept her from moving. In the year her family had been living here, the little lighthouse had done its job well, guiding boats into Scituate harbor and warning ships bound for Boston, twenty-five miles up the coast, to stay away from this rocky shore. She had not seen a wreck, and Pa had not had to risk his life— until tonight.

"We are here to save lives, Rebecca," Pa reminded her gently but firmly. "Make sure the line is secure."

She did so while he hurried to the rowboat that lay upside down on the beach. The rope's other end was tied to an iron ring at the rowboat's bow. With a grunt Pa turned the boat over and began hauling it to the edge of the water.

Rebecca's eight-year-old sister Abigail came running out to the beach. "I heard the cannon," Abigail said. "What's Pa doing, Becky?"

"There's a boat in trouble out there, Abby. Look."

The dory's mast had begun to splinter and its front end was already underwater.

"Whatever happens," Pa called to the girls,

"stay on the shore. The current is too strong for you." He shoved the boat into the water, then jumped aboard and began rowing.

Pa's lifeline wound out slowly. Struggling against the waves, the rowboat would point almost straight up, then smash down into the hollows. Finally it bumped up next to the fishing boat. Pa pulled his oars aboard and leaned over. Pushing aside a tangle of sailcloth on the dory, he hoisted out a limp body.

The rowboat dipped low and a wave sloshed in, making it tilt lower still. Pa lost his grip on the body, which fell into the sea and sank. Quickly, he untied the rope from its iron ring and looped it around his waist. Then, pulling off his shoes, he dove in.

The girls gasped as the lifeline uncoiled in a zinging blur. Pa's head broke the surface far from shore. He started to shout something but then the lifeline, stretched to its full length, snapped. Rebecca ran to catch it—too late. It went skittering across the beach toward the waves.

She stopped and looked out. In the calm glow of the lighthouse she could see that the wrecked dory and the rowboat had both been swept out to sea, leaving behind only a few jagged planks.

And Pa was gone.

2 The Dark Ship

Rebecca and Abigail stood frozen in their tracks before the foaming sea.

"Pa?" Abigail whispered.

Suddenly, Pa popped up, wheezing and thrashing. Rebecca rushed toward the waves.

"Becky!" her sister called.

She stopped.

"We're supposed to stay on the shore," Abigail reminded her. "Pa said," she added tearfully.

"We have to do *something*," Rebecca complained. In frustration she kicked at a stone near her feet, stubbing her toe and nearly tripping on the lifeline.

The lifeline! It had snagged on a big rock near the water's edge.

"Pa!" Rebecca shouted. "Hang on!"

She couldn't tell if he heard or not, but she

began pulling on the rope anyway. A wave shoved him closer and the line grew slack. Then the wave receded, trying to suck him out with it, and the line snapped taut. Rebecca's arms felt as if they would tear off at the shoulders. "Abby," she cried, "help!"

Abigail rushed up behind Rebecca and grabbed onto the rope as another wave smashed toward shore. Pa disappeared under a rolling wall of water. The wave curled, broke and retreated. All of a sudden Pa was staggering up onto the seaweed-slick rocks. He lay down the limp form he was carrying, then collapsed.

Dropping the rope, the girls rushed over to him. They helped him sit up and asked if he was all right. He nodded, coughing.

"Don't worry about me," he said through chattering teeth. "We have to take care of that fellow."

They turned the face-down figure over.

"Why, it's Jacob Webster," Pa said. "That old fisherman knows these waters as well as anyone. What would make him steer onto the rocks? Jacob, can you hear me?"

Jacob Webster groaned.

"We'd all best get inside," Pa said, untying the rope from his waist.

Moving Mr. Webster was not easy. He was a big

man, and his scratchy, waterlogged sweater didn't help. Grunting and tugging, Pa and the girls managed to get him up to the cottage.

By the glow of an oil lamp on the kitchen counter they could see a bruise beneath Mr. Webster's white hair. His eyelids fluttered when Pa sat him down in one of the straight-back chairs.

"I saw..." he mumbled.

"You just rest easy," Pa told him.

"No...have to warn..." Mr. Webster slumped over.

Pa turned to Rebecca. "I will lay him on my bed. You go put the cannon and rope away, then check the lights. Abigail, go with her and help. Come right back in when you're done. I may need you."

Outside, the top of the tower was glowing brightly. A few lights glimmered in Scituate, the village across the harbor. Once the girls had coiled the lifeline and wheeled the little cannon back into the shed, Abigail turned toward the cottage. But Rebecca lingered, scanning the waves.

"Pa said to come right back in, Becky," Abigail reminded her.

"In a minute."

"You always say something like that." Abigail studied her sister for a long moment. Finally she asked in a curious tone, "What are you doing?"

"Looking for the rowboat. Maybe it washed up somewhere and we can save it."

"But Pa said—"

"Abby, look over there." Rebecca saw something. But it was not the rowboat. There was a shape out on the water, low and dark, beyond the light-house's halo. She could almost make out other shapes rising up from it, tall and spindly, like masts. "Do you see that?"

Abigail looked where she was pointing. "See what?"

"It looks like a ship," Rebecca said. "But with no lights."

"I don't see anything. Doesn't a ship have to have lamps lit at night?"

"Unless she's abandoned, or..." The dark shape drifted out of view, and now the sea's surface was empty. "Or she doesn't want anybody to know she's there."

"We'd better tell Pa," Abigail said.

They found him in the kitchen, dressed in dry clothes and sipping from a mug. He had gotten a fire going in the pot-bellied stove in the corner and now the room smelled comfortingly of coffee and woodsmoke. From the bedroom off the kitchen came the sound of Mr. Webster's snoring. Keeping her voice low, Rebecca described the dark

24

shape and the masts.

"All right," Pa said. "I'll have a look."

"May I come with you, Pa?" Rebecca asked.

"You need your rest. Both of you. You have done well this evening but now you need to get some sleep."

Abigail crossed the narrow parlor. Rebecca watched Pa go out the door, then followed her sister up the ladder to the loft. She placed her fife carefully on the dresser next to the slate she and Abigail used for spelling and sums. The girls slipped into long flannel nightgowns and lay down in their beds.

"Becky, did you get scared tonight?" Abigail asked, her voice quivering.

"Just a bit, I suppose," Rebecca told her. "But I knew nothing would happen to Pa." This was not exactly true, but she knew her little sister needed to hear it. In fact, so did Rebecca herself. Just thinking about what might have happened tonight made her tremble.

Within moments she heard Abigail breathing deeply in her sleep. But every time she closed her eyes, the sight of Pa floundering in the surf came back to her.

She got up. Careful not to bang her head on the slanted ceiling, she tiptoed to the loft's window.

Light from the tower and the moon danced on the ocean. How thrilled she had been last year when her family had moved to this cozy cottage on the shore. Her father, one of the most respected men in Scituate, had been appointed by President James Madison himself to be the first keeper of the lighthouse on Cedar Point. That meant he would be staying home, not gone for months the way he had been when he was a sea captain. Rebecca remembered standing on the dock with Ma and Abigail, watching his ship until its masts disappeared below the horizon. They never knew when—or even if—he would be back.

Yet tonight, only a few yards from land and right before her eyes, the sea had almost taken him. And as if that weren't enough, there had been that ship, low and dark and mysterious.

When she heard Pa come in she climbed down to the parlor. He was lighting a fire. Sparks flew up as he tossed a log into the wide fireplace.

"Rebecca?" he asked, looking over his shoulder. "What is the matter? I didn't see any ship, if that's what you are wondering."

"No," she said. "I mean yes. I mean, well, we almost..." Her voice cracked. "We almost lost you tonight, Pa."

"Not likely. Especially with you around to help."

26

He settled into his rocking chair by the hearth, then held out his arms for her. She snuggled into his lap and they sat listening to the embers crackling, the clock ticking on the mantle, the waves pounding outside. Rebecca felt a glow that had nothing to do with the burning logs.

"Off to bed now," Pa finally said. "I have to go check the lights."

Rebecca gave him a last, long hug, then climbed back up the ladder. Warm beneath her quilt, she was soon asleep.

3 Yankee Doodle

Hazy morning light came in through the window. Rebecca lay half-awake, gazing up at the rafters and thinking it was time to go spoon out the apple butter and put some johnnycakes on the griddle for breakfast the way Ma had taught her. In a minute, she told herself, stretching and yawning and listening to the calls of the seabirds. Then someone began making noise down in the parlor. She tossed aside her quilt, tiptoed to the edge of the loft, and listened.

"Don't you lecture me about how I had no business going fishing on my own," Jacob Webster was saying. "I may be old, Simeon Bates, but I can still haul my trawl good as any man. I can still see, too, and I am telling you I saw a big ship out there. Prowling around with no lights lit, she was."

Abigail leaned down next to Rebecca. "What's

31

going on, Becky?" she whispered. Rebecca shushed her.

"The girls thought they saw a ship like that, too," Pa told Jacob Webster. "I watched for it all night but I didn't see—"

"It's the British, I tell you," Mr. Webster said.

Rebecca and Abigail looked at each other.

"Where was this ship heading, Jacob?" Pa asked. "Did you see what course she—"

"I knew I had to get away in a hurry. Had to go warn somebody just like Paul Revere did back in '75."

"Jacob."

"I met him once, you know."

"Yes, I know. Jacob?"

"Why, if he was around today—"

"Jacob!"

"What *is* it, Simeon?"

"The ship. Where was she heading?"

"How should I know? I swung back toward land fast as I could—so quick I fell and hit my fool head on the mast. That is the last thing I remember."

"You know," Pa said, "I saw a fire over in the village around dawn. I wonder if that ship had anything to do with—"

"You mean them British came ashore *here*? What has kept you so busy that you haven't gone

32

and told somebody about that ship?'"

There was a pause. "Tending the light and looking after a half-drowned fisherman I had to rescue," Pa said dryly.

"Bah! Why are we sitting around *now*? Call out the militia! Summon the army! Send for the—"

"Now, Jacob. We both know a fire can start for any number of reasons. I'll go over to Scituate and look into it while you stay here and rest."

"Rest?" Mr. Webster fumed. "Not on your life. I am going with you."

"Are you sure you are feeling well enough to walk the mile over to town?"

"As sure as my socks smell like old fish. Let's go."

Pa walked over to the ladder, his footsteps muffled by the parlor's braided rug. "You two listening?" he called up.

"Yes, Pa," Abigail admitted.

"Thought you might be. Get yourselves dressed. We are going to the village."

After a quick breakfast they set out in the cool morning, following a track through the cedar forest lining the shore. The sea-weedy smell of low tide mixed with the crisp scent of the trees. In a while they came out of the woods and began crossing a cornfield belonging to a neighboring farm. Trees lightly touched by autumn reds and golds stood on the hills in the distance.

Suddenly, marching music began drifting over from the direction of the village.

"Sounds as if someone has already sent for help," Pa said. "That's the militia we are hearing, if I am not mistaken."

They hurried the rest of the way into town, past the little shops and over to the common, where it seemed all of Scituate had gathered. When Rebecca squeezed through the cheering crowd she saw armed men coming. There were about twenty of them, marching to "Yankee Doodle" on fife and drum. The instruments were larger than Rebecca's and Abigail's, so the fife sounded wonderfully full, the drum wonderfully deep.

Rebecca recognized several men from Scituate who had gone off last summer to join a militia unit called the Home Guard. Leading the way was James Bristow, the village postmaster, who now wore the blue uniform of an army officer. The rest were wearing cotton shirts or buckskin jackets. All carried muskets. A dust cloud settled behind them as they tramped onto the common.

Mrs. Russell from the bakery came up to Pa. "Simeon, did you hear about George Fiedler's boatyard?" she asked. "It burned to the ground this morning. And the folks who put out the fire saw men in uniform running away."

Jacob Webster let out an I-told-you-so grunt. "That would be just like them British," he muttered, "creeping around in the dark like that. They probably sneaked ashore someplace where they couldn't be seen from the lighthouse."

"You may be right, Jacob," Pa said. "Let's go talk with Colonel Bristow."

"May Abby and I stay here, Pa?" Rebecca asked.

"All right, but don't wander off."

The girls watched as the fifer and drummer sounded out signals. One signal made the men run forward; another made them drop to their knees and take aim with their muskets; yet another made them rise and get back into line. They began marching around to "Yankee Doodle" once more.

Abigail tugged on Rebecca's sleeve. "Do you think we could do that?" she asked.

"Do what, Abby?"

"Play music like them. It is such a wonderful tune."

"I suppose," Rebecca said without enthusiasm.

Rebecca saw Abigail look down. She felt badly, but then, they *had* tried playing music together once or twice. All her sister could do was pound out the simplest of beats. Rebecca had more fun playing by herself.

Then Pa was back. "They've trained well, our Home Guard, haven't they?" he said. "Colonel Bristow says they will stay here for a while. The British sailors aren't prepared to fight on land, so we will be safe. Mr. Webster is heading home. We should do the same."

The only thing unusual about the next several days was the sound of the militia's fife and drum drifting across the harbor to Cedar Point, but that made all seem well. A neighbor brought some pumpkins, and Rebecca showed Abigail how to make pudding from them, a spicy treat to look forward to with their noontime dinner. A letter came from Ma. She said she missed them and promised to be home before long.

Then one morning they awoke to a dense fog that clung to their skin and hid the sea, muffling the sound of the waves. Sailors would be in danger out there because they could not see the rocky coast. While Pa worked in the tiny, round lamp-room to keep the lights shining through the fog, Rebecca stood on the tower's porch and tugged the bell cord a couple of times a minute. She was glad to be outside; even after a year, she had not gotten used to the stench of burning whale oil. But it was hard to stay alert staring into the mist. She occupied herself by humming "Yankee Doodle" and trying to imagine how to finger the tune on her fife.

When the fog finally lifted that afternoon and the ocean was sparkling with sunlight, she climbed down the tower, stood at the water's edge, and took the fife from her apron pocket. With just a little trial and error she was playing "Yankee Doodle." What a fine, bouncy tune it was! Then she remembered how much her sister had liked it, too. She supposed she really ought to share it with Abigail.

Rebecca found her sweeping out the parlor and asked if she was still interested in playing the song. Abigail's face lit up, but only for a moment.

"I have to finish my sweeping," she said.

"Finish in a hurry, then."

Abigail did so, then ran to fetch her little drum from the loft. The girls went to the beach and started in on "Yankee Doodle." Abigail's drum made only a thin sound, nothing like the pounding thuds of the Home Guard's drum, but at least she kept time. Gradually, though, her drum beats grew more confident, which inspired Rebecca to try to make her fife sound better. Then, after a verse or two, something special seemed to enter the music. The girls could tell, by just nodding or winking at each other, that they should play a bit louder in this passage or more quietly through that one. Yes, Rebecca had always enjoyed playing the fife, but what was happening now, with two people playing, was incredible. What a difference Abigail's drum made. The song had come alive, and Rebecca wanted it to last forever.

On the far side of the harbor the Home Guard played as if in response. The girls smiled at one another. Loose stones by the water's edge rattled against each other when the waves crashed across them and fell back. It sounded just like a clapping crowd, as if the sea itself were applauding.

But then Rebecca heard another sound—or rather the lack of another sound. It took a moment to realize what was happening. She stopped blowing into her fife and stood still, listening to the militia's music growing faint.

"What is wrong, Becky?" Abigail asked, letting her drumming trail off. Then she heard the fading song from the other side of the harbor. "Oh," she said. "Are the soldiers marching away?"

"It sounds that way," Rebecca said. "Come on, Abby," she went on, hoping she sounded more confident than she felt. "We should get the washing started."

Abigail blinked. She seemed speechless that Rebecca had actually suggested they get back to chores. Without a word she turned and carried her drum to the cottage. Rebecca followed, lingering, listening, hearing now only the surf and the gulls.

They scrubbed the clothes in a wooden tub in the kitchen, wrung them out, and hung them outside to dry. Then Rebecca went over to where Pa was applying some fresh whitewash to the tower. "Pa," she asked, "why did the Home Guard leave?"

He lowered his brush and wiped his brow. "They have the whole coast to patrol, Rebecca."

Then Rebecca asked, "Do you think the British will come back now?"

"Well, Colonel Bristow told me he would keep his men here until he was sure everything was all right, so we just have to assume everything *is* fine."

Later, Rebecca went about her chores—dusting the cottage, sweeping out the shed, stirring the fish chowder that simmered in a kettle on the stove. She stole glances through any window facing the ocean. Aside from the usual schooners and dories, she saw no ship.

That evening, she helped get Abigail ready for bed.

"You're worried about the soldiers leaving, aren't you?" Abigail asked as she drew up her covers.

Rebecca hesitated. "I didn't think you could tell."

Abigail waited.

"Yes, I suppose I am a little worried," Rebecca admitted. "But Pa says everything will be fine. So let's try not to worry, all right?"

"All right. Becky, will you sing me a song?"

"I don't really know any songs."

"You must," Abigail protested. "What about those songs Ma sings for us?"

"I don't know the words."

Abigail was quiet. "I miss Ma," she finally said.

"I do, too." Rebecca paused. "I suppose I could try. What song do you want?"

Abigail named several soft old ballads. Rebecca started in on one, stumbled over the verses, and then saw a mischievous look cross her sister's face. Abigail came in with some made-up verses of her own, silly lyrics that soon had both of them giggling. Rebecca looked at Abigail in wonder. Her sister was growing up, becoming something besides the quiet little girl she had always seemed to be.

Even so, it was time for bed. Rebecca tucked her

in, climbed down from the loft, and walked over to the lighthouse. Footsteps echoing out the hatchway, she scaled the winding wooden staircase, then hoisted herself up the ladder to the lamp-room.

Pa was pouring whale oil into the round brass reservoir that hung by chains from the ceiling. Rebecca got busy polishing the glass tubes around the rim of the reservoir that held the wicks. Of course, Pa had done that earlier when he snuffed out the lights, but the flakes of black, oily soot always seemed to come back by themselves. In a while the wicks were trimmed and lit, the brass and glass were gleaming, and the lamp-room was bright and warm. Pa and Rebecca could see only their own reflections in the tall windows.

Rebecca climbed down the tower with an empty oil cask. Near the bottom she glanced out the hatchway. A rowboat, bigger than Pa's, was pulled up on the beach. Offshore, glowing in the lighthouse's halo, a huge ship was anchored. Its bow rode high above the water, its three masts looked like a grove of winter trees, and its sides were studded with cannon barrels.

Rebecca heard footsteps behind her. Turning, she saw shadowy figures coming through the shed toward her. One wore the plumed hat of a naval

41

commander. The sword hanging from his belt scraped on the granite floor as he entered the lighthouse.

"Might there be any adults here?" he asked, his deep voice echoing eerily on the stone walls. But it was his accent that frightened her, one she had heard old-timers imitate when they were telling stories about the Revolution. A British accent.

"Adults," the man repeated. "Are there any here, girl?"

"Yes," Rebecca managed to say.

"Be so good as to fetch one. Now."

Rebecca dropped the cask and ran up the stairs.

4 The Enemy

Rebecca returned with Pa.

"I am Captain Farris of His Majesty's Ship *La Hache*," said the British officer.

"What do you want, Captain?" Pa asked. He had one hand on Rebecca's shoulder. With his other he held up a lantern. The jackets of the British sailors were an angry red in the flickering light.

"We have not been able to put in to shore for some time," Captain Farris said. "Soldiers and ships patrolling the coast, you know. This isolated town, however, will do nicely."

"For what?" Pa asked.

"For supplies, of course, which you shall furnish."

"We have soldiers here, Captain," Pa said.

"Indeed, sir? We saw them marching away this

45

afternoon," added Captain Farris.

"How could you?" Rebecca asked. "You were never close enough. We would have seen you."

"Men raise dust when they march, young lady. We could see the cloud from out on the water. So we knew that you were unprotected here. Now, we require lumber and canvas, plus fresh water, of course, and enough food to feed my crew for the next several weeks."

"You are the enemy," Pa said evenly. "Why should we do this for you?"

"Surely you realize it was men from the *La Hache* who burned that boatyard the other night."

"Do you expect that will make us want to help you?" Pa asked.

"I expect you to understand that your nation and mine are at war, sir," the captain snapped. Then he softened his tone. "Sometimes, unfortunately, doing my duty means that I must order the burning of a boatyard that could build ships for your navy. That was all we intended to do here, but now we find we are running out of supplies. Tell me, sir, have you served aboard a ship?"

"I was a captain," Pa said.

"Then you understand that I must be responsible for my vessel and my crew. I am sending some of them into the town now to secure those supplies. Others will remain here. We shall need to keep an eye on you while we go about our business so that you do not run off to summon your soldiers. Please come with me."

The sailors led Pa and Rebecca through the shed and out into the night. At Captain Farris's direction, one of the British took the lantern from Pa and began swinging it back and forth. A longboat was hoisted then over the side of the *La Hache*. As the little craft settled onto the waves, men began swarming down rope ladders slung from the warship's rail. They climbed into the longboat and started rowing toward shore, oars swinging up and down as one.

"You must realize," Pa told the captain, "that the villagers will not give you what you want without a fight."

"That," Captain Farris said, "is why my men will inform them that you are my...my guests. You and the little girl."

"No," Pa said.

"No harm shall come to you—if you and the villagers cooperate with us." The captain turned to his men. "See that these two are rowed out to the *La Hache* and held there. We may need to use them again. Once the supplies are handed over, burn anything in the town that looks as if it might be useful to the American navy."

Two of the sailors grabbed Pa's arms. The others came for Rebecca.

"Run, Rebecca!" Pa shouted. "Run!"

Hands reached out for her. She ducked, then pushed past them. With Pa still shouting at her to run, she raced across the beach. The loose, round rocks tripped her. Regaining her balance, she plunged into the forest. A big root caught her foot and she fell, landing heavily on moss. Over her own heavy breathing she heard footsteps running after her. She crawled next to a cedar and pressed herself against its shaggy bark.

Soon there were men all around her, crashing through the forest, thrashing at the branches, searching for her.

She held her breath.

One sailor was so near that she could see the ragged cuffs of his white trousers. He came closer, stopped, came closer still, closer…

Then Captain Farris's voice rang out from over by the lighthouse. "We have no time for this," he shouted. "Leave her."

The men crashed out of the forest and all was still. Rebecca lay shivering for what seemed a very long time. She hated herself for running away. Yes, Pa had told her to, but even so she wondered if she should have stayed to help. Perhaps she could run to the village now, warn everyone that the sailors were coming. But what then? There would be fighting, shooting, killing. And what if the British caught her before she even got there? What would they do to her? To Pa?

Then another, more terrible thought struck her: Abigail! She had left her sister sleeping in the cottage. What if Abigail woke up and made noise or lit a lamp? What if—oh please, no—what if the British went looking in the cottage?

Rebecca picked herself up and stole to the edge of the forest. She peered around a tree just in time to see Pa being led toward the rowboat on the beach. No one seemed to have gone near the cottage.

She crouched low, raced over to the little house, and charged through the door. The kitchen was empty and cold. She dashed across the parlor and pulled herself up the ladder to the loft.

Abigail was kneeling by the window, peeking out. When she heard Rebecca behind her she yelped.

"Shh!" Rebecca said. "It's me, Abby."

"Oh, Becky! I heard all different voices. What's going on? Why is that ship out there?"

"It's the British," Rebecca whispered, coming up

to the window. "They have Pa and they are going to burn the town."

Abigail gasped. "Becky, I'm so scared."

"So am I." Rebecca looked out. Another longboat had set forth from the ship.

"I wish we could do something to scare them back," Abigail whispered.

"There's nothing we can do," Rebecca told her. "See where they're going?" The first boat was moving toward the beach. The other steered into the harbor. "They're sneaking up on the town from land and sea."

"If only the Home Guard were here."

"Even if they weren't. If they were just coming and you could hear them in the distance. The music alone would..." She cut herself off and looked at her sister.

"Would what, Becky?"

"Would do what you said you wanted to do. Scare them." Rebecca turned back to the window. Two sailors were pushing Pa into the rowboat. Out on the water the men in the first longboat had lifted their oars and were letting the waves carry them to the beach. The other longboat was far into the harbor now. There might still be time—not much, but maybe enough.

Breathlessly, Rebecca explained her plan.

50

"What if it doesn't work?" Abigail asked.

"Pa says we are here to save lives. We have to try. Please."

Chin quaking, Abigail nodded. The girls grabbed what they needed, then rushed down the ladder.

5 Abigail's Drum

Rebecca chanced a quick look out the door and made sure no one was coming toward the cottage. She took Abigail by the hand. Together they raced over to the lighthouse and hid behind the tower.

Peeking around the side, Rebecca saw that the British were already moving up the beach.

"Ready?" Rebecca whispered.

"Ready," Abigail whispered back. But she did not begin.

"Now!" Rebecca urged.

Abigail lifted her drumsticks, then pounded once, softly, on the head of her little drum.

"Come on," Rebecca hissed.

Again Abigail pounded once, a bit louder. Then, taking a deep breath, she launched into a shaky rhythm. The drum's sound was pitifully small.

Her lips dry, Rebecca began to blow on the fife.

"Yankee Doodle" limped out, rough and breathy and full of mistakes. She could barely hear the fife and drum over the crashing of the waves. When the song was done she looked around the side of the tower.

The British had stopped moving.

"Did you hear that?" one of them yelled. "The American soldiers must be coming back!"

"*That* noise?" another yelled. "That sounded like a sick seagull. Keep marching."

They started coming again.

The plan had failed!

No time to retreat to the cottage now. The girls dashed inside the shed and headed for the darkness beneath the tower's steps. Their footsteps clacked on the stone floor, echoing so loudly that Rebecca was sure the British would hear them. If only the hatchway didn't throw sound all over the beach.

Sound! All over the beach!

Rebecca stood and looked out. The British were only a few yards away.

"What are you doing?" Abigail whispered.

"Come over here, Abby, and start playing again."

"But they will hear us."

"Of course they'll hear us. If the plan works at

56

all, it will work because of your drum. I can't do this by myself. Please. Start playing."

Abigail began playing. The walls echoed the noise, making her sound like a whole troop of drummers. She looked up, a delighted smile on her face. Her pounding grew loud and steady.

Rebecca began piping "Yankee Doodle." It didn't matter that her playing was still shaky or that the fife was so small. The walls made her sound just fine.

Rebecca and Abigail went all the way through the song, then started again, louder and faster, as if fife and drum were trying to drown each other out. By now Rebecca wasn't making any mistakes. She and her sister sounded so much like the militia that even she was ready to believe the Home Guard was coming.

Rebecca looked out the hatchway. The men on the beach had stopped marching and were looking at each other in confusion. But they did not retreat. Rebecca blew harder, which made Abigail pound harder. All of a sudden some of the British began to sprint back toward the longboat.

Pa broke loose from his guards and darted up toward the lighthouse. Two sailors chased him, but they began running back down the beach when they heard the music up close. Along with several others, they helped shove the longboat into the water, then climbed aboard and began rowing for the *La Hache.*

Rebecca felt as if she had blown all the air out of her lungs. She could tell from Abigail's slumped shoulders and wobbly arms that her sister felt exhausted too. But a few sailors remained on the beach, including Captain Farris, who was yelling at his men to stand their ground. The girls kept playing.

Pa raced past the lighthouse, shouting a welcome to Colonel Bristow. He must have realized then that the Home Guard troops were not there—and that the noise was coming from *inside* the tower. He came up to the hatchway.

"Hello, Pa," Abigail said without missing a beat.

His eyes bulged open and his jaw dropped halfway to his chest.

Out in the harbor, the boat that had been heading toward town slowed, then stopped, then turned around.

"The village!" Captain Farris bellowed. "Row to the village!"

By now Pa had recovered himself. "I know what might change the captain's mind," he said. "Keep playing. Just keep playing." He raced around to the shed. A moment later—

BOOM!

Rebecca and Abigail stopped playing. But they weren't the only ones startled by the signal cannon.

The few men left on the beach dove into the rowboat and pulled away from shore—so quickly that they almost left Captain Farris behind. Tripping on his sword, he stumbled into the surf. The rowboat nearly capsized as its crew hoisted him aboard. Then they rowed back to the warship.

Pa appeared in the hatchway. "Now we have to hope they don't fire back," he said. "Better play some more."

The girls played faster and louder.

But the British were in a hurry to get away. The landing party scrambled back onto the *La Hache* without even bothering to get the small boats aboard. Abigail and Rebecca kept sounding out "Yankee Doodle" as the warship raised its anchor and set sail. Only then did they put down their instruments and collapse against the cool stone walls.

"Who would have believed it?" Pa said, laughing and shaking his head. "The plan worked because of Abigail's drum." "But it was Becky's idea," Abigail said.

"Well," Pa responded. "I guess you girls are an army of two."

They all went to the hatchway and watched as the warship, gliding majestically over the waves, sailed out of the lighthouse's halo. Pa put an arm around each of his daughters and led them out of the lighthouse. The surf crashed and the gulls cried and the tower glowed calmly as they walked safely back to the cottage.

Word about what the girls had done spread quickly through Scituate. Over the next several days they were obliged to play "Yankee Doodle" for each of the many well-wishers who came streaming out to Cedar Point. Jacob Webster sailed across the harbor one morning to show off his new dory, one of the British longboats that he'd found washed up near the village and had fitted with a mast. He was towing the British rowboat, which he had also salvaged.

"The rowboat is a present for you, Simeon," Mr. Webster called when he stepped ashore. "Next time use a stronger rope." Then he made the girls play their song. He even smiled—almost—and made them play it again.

Afterward, lips and fingers numb, Rebecca took Pa aside. "Would it be all right," she asked, "if we just did chores for a while?"

Afterword

Afterword

This story was inspired by an actual event. After the American colonies won their independence from England, the two countries argued about whether the United States could expand its territory and do business with nations other than England. War broke out in the summer of 1812. Being young and weak, America was unprepared, leaving the British free to raid the New England coast.

No one knows for sure when they tried to come ashore at Scituate (pronounced "SIT-chew-it," by the way). But many different sources agree that Rebecca and Abigail Bates, daughters of the keeper of the light on Cedar Point, really did use fife and drum to frighten the British away. In her later years, Rebecca wrote letters in which she described the event. Quite a few people already knew about it from articles and drawings in several popular magazines, so she was able to sell these letters to raise money for her family.

Scituate Light had its troubles over the years. Planners argued for months about where to locate it, then discovered after it was built that it wasn't tall enough to be seen far out at sea. It never had a proper fog bell, either. I put the small bell in the tower to move the story along, though at least one lighthouse at the time did have something like this. It's possible that Mr. Bates would have used a fog *trumpet* instead, but I just couldn't have him trying to warn Jacob Webster with a noise like a wounded elephant.

The tower's height was doubled in the 1830's. Since all the good granite in the area had been used in the original tower, the builders had to use bricks made of sand. These began crumbling almost immediately and still need constant attention.

The cottage, however, has survived well. It was built of "King's Wood," first-rate lumber that would have been sent to England if the Revolution had not taken place. A little crown branded into the wood is visible in some of the house's timbers.

Other improvements to the lighthouse included a red-lensed light that shone in a row of windows beneath the lamp-room. This was an attempt to make Scituate Light look different from the one at Boston (every lighthouse has a unique signal and markings so mariners can tell where they are). A Fresnel ("fruh-NELL") lens was installed in the 1850's. Named for the French scientist who invented it, this sophisticated prism greatly boosted the beam's power. In fact, it had to be covered by a black felt cloth during the day so it would not ignite fires with magnified sunlight. A clockwork mechanism made the lens rotate so that a shaded portion covered the lamps every few seconds. This made the beam appear to blink. Now sailors could distinguish the lighthouse from the steady lights of other boats, which made their voyage safer.

Rebecca's nephew was the last government-appointed

keeper of the light. When a more up-to-date lighthouse was built nearby in the 1860's, Scituate Light was shut down. Dark for many years, it is, fortunately, now lit once more. Though beachfront homes crowd Cedar Point today, the waters there remain treacherous. A few years ago a Greek freighter went aground near the lighthouse during a storm. When she was repaired and refloated, her crew, as called for by the customs of the sea, renamed her the *Scituate*, thus honoring a town that still works hard to keep the seas safe.

Thanks to George and Ruth Downton, the keepers at Scituate Light, who showed me around, told me wonderful tales about the place, and let me hold the fife Rebecca played; to my research assistant Emily Smith; and to my editor, Barbara Francis.